Sofia Makes a Friend

Written by Catherine Hapka

Illustrated by Character Building Studio
and the Disney Storybook Art Team

DISNEP PRESS

New York • Los Angeles

For information address Disney Press, 1101 Flower Street, Glendale, California 91201.

ISBN 978-1-4847-1336-5
F383-2370-2-14129
Printed in China
First Box Set Edition, 2014
1 3 5 7 9 10 8 6 4 2

For more Disney Press fun, visit www.disneybooks.com

Not for individual resale.

 is excited.
Sofia

Royal visitors are coming

to the  !
palace

"King Baldric and Queen Ada
will be here soon," says Queen
Miranda.

"Our visitors are bringing a special guest," says King Roland. "I hope you will help her feel at home in our ."

palace

"The special guest is probably a princess," Amber whispers to  Sofia.

5

A 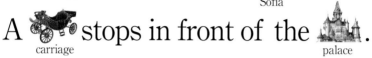 sounds.

"The guests are here!" Sofia cries.

A carriage stops in front of the palace.

Two people get out of the  .
"Where is the princess?" Amber
wonders.

carriage

Then a baby  jumps out of
the !
Queen Ada smiles.

8

"This is our new pet  unicorn .
Her name is Pearl.
I hope you won't mind watching
her for us."

"Oh!"  Sofia cries. "Pearl is so cute!"

"Her  horn is pretty," Amber says.

"It will be fun to watch her!"

Sofia , Amber, and James take Pearl

for a walk.

Pearl chases the  birds and eats

the flowers .

Pearl jumps into the  .
fountain

She shakes off next to Amber.

"Hey!" Amber cries. "Stop that!"

13

"I know," James says.

"Pearl can watch us play ."
horseshoes

He throws a .
horseshoe

Pearl catches the  and brings
horseshoe

it back to James.

"Hey! She ruined my throw!"

James says.

Amber has another idea.
"We can play dress-up.

Pearl will look cute in a pretty
hat and tutu."
Pearl takes a big bite
out of Amber's hat.

"No, Pearl!" Amber cries.

She tries to grab the .
hat

But the unicorn runs away.

Pearl runs through the .
  palace

She jumps on the  and nibbles
  piano

on a .
  tapestry

"Watching Pearl is no fun," James says.

"She ruins everything," Amber adds.

Pearl hears them talking.

Her head droops. Her  goes dull.
horn

She runs and hides behind a  .
tapestry

"We said we would help Pearl feel at home in our palace,"

Sofia reminds the others.

"But she does not like to do
any of the things we like to do!"
Amber says.

That gives 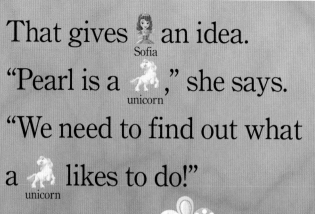 an idea.
Sofia

"Pearl is a ," she says.
unicorn

"We need to find out what

a  likes to do!"
unicorn

 can hear and talk to animals.

 tells Pearl her secret.

"What do you like to do?" she asks.

"I love 🎵," says Pearl.
music

 leads the  over to where Pearl is hiding.
The  play a lively tune.

Sofia   palace   musicians   musicians

 Sofia, Amber, and James dance and sing along with the 🎵 music. The tapestry moves....

Then Pearl jumps out!
She looks happy, and her pretty  shines again.

horn

"Hooray!"  Sofia cheers.

"We made Pearl feel at home

in our palace."

"Because you figured out what
she likes to do."
James smiles at  Sofia.
"And it's fun for us, too!"

The rest of the visit
is filled with  and fun.

music

, Amber, and James can't wait

Sofia

for Pearl's next visit!